# Ten Tiny Turtles
## A Crazy Counting Book

## Paul Cherrill

Copyright © 1995 by Paul Cherrill
First American edition 1995 published by
Ticknor & Fields Books for Young Readers
A Houghton Mifflin Company, 215 Park Avenue South,
New York, New York 10003.

First published in Great Britain by Methuen Childrens Books, an imprint of
Reed Consumer Books Ltd.
Manufactured in Hong Kong.

Library of Congress Cataloging-in-Publication Data

Cherrill, Paul,
    Ten Tiny Turtles / by Paul Cherrill. – 1st American ed.
    p.   cm.
    Summary: All kinds of animals, from a water-squirting dog to ten
    tiny turtles in T-shirts, illustrate the numbers from one to ten.
                ISBN 0-395-71250-5
    [1.Animals-Fiction. 2. Counting. 3. Stories in rhyme.]
            I. Title  II. Title: 10 tiny turtles.
PZ8.3.C426TE  1995
[E]-dc20                                      94-19904
                                                CIP
                                                AC

# Ten Tiny Turtles
## A Crazy Counting Book

# Paul Cherrill

Ticknor & Fields Books for Young Readers
New York 1995

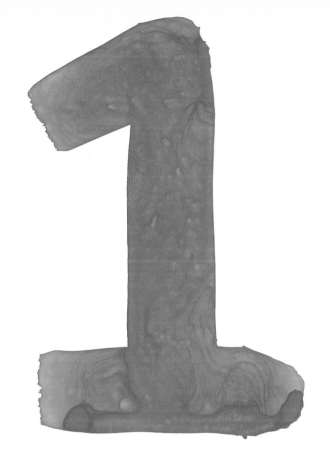

One playful dog
squirting water
at the cat

**2**

Two rabbits dancing~
how about
that

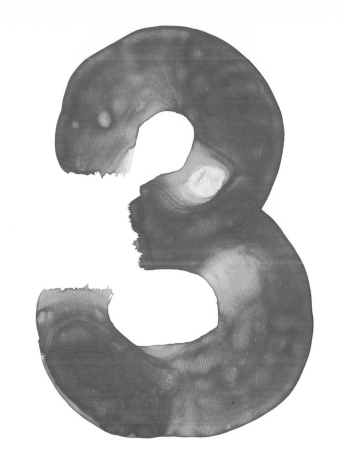

Three pies baked by the rat dressed for dinner

**4**

Four bottles of Pop
for the chicken
race Winner

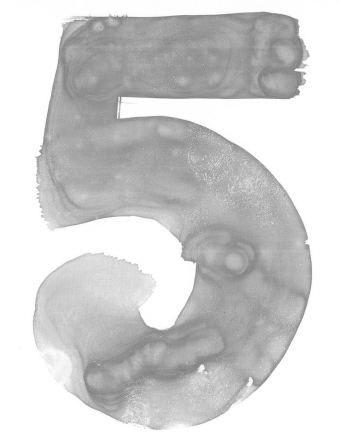

5

Five fluffy sheep
pretending to
be clouds

# Six slim cats standing tall and looking proud

# 7

Seven slimy worms
wearing glasses
in the sun

Eight spotted fish
Playing hockey
Just for fun

# 9

Nine noisy bees
for the fat toad
to catch

# 10

# Ten tiny turtles wearing T-shirts that match